THE KINDNESS CLUB

Bright Light

Hardie Grant Children's Publishing

Kate Bullen-Casanova

Dave Petzold

Welcome to the Kindness Club!
Hello there, you must be new.
I'm Oliver, what's your name?
Come on, I'll look after you.

Over here are the cubbies
to store our bags, hats and shoes.

There's so much we can do here.
Best of all – we're free to choose!

Let's follow the garden path
up to my favourite space.
Our group-time mat is laid out
to honour this special place.

Gather all our friends around.
Some days we read a book,

or have a morning disco,
dancing proudly – come and look!

Here at the Kindness Club,
we all help prepare our snack.
Fruit and veggies for us all,
plus the chickens out the back!

We love to work together,
building towers with our blocks.
Rainy days mean inside play,
searching in the dress-up box.

We paint in all the colours
and make monsters
with playdough.

When you're done with that big puzzle,
may I please have a go?

Let's see what's for lunch today …
Pasta! Yay! It's time to eat!

We'll wash our hands up at the sink.
Come with me, let's find a seat.

Here at the Kindness Club,
we use our superpowers!
We cuddle dolls, drive diggers,
play soccer and grow flowers.

Queens on horses, climbing trees,
mixing up a muddy mess.
Beep beep! We are coming through …
in crowns and a fancy dress!

Helmets on and off we go –
zoom quickly through the puddle!

Oh no! Are you okay, my friend?
Or would you like a cuddle?

Here at the Kindness Club,
all that matters is you try.
When we're feeling sad or hurt,
we know that it's brave to cry.

Whisper now, we're in the fort,
gently settle down to rest.
And here – if you're feeling scared,
borrow teddy, he's the best.

With helping hands we tidy
and put all the toys away,
now that we have reached the end
of another lovely day.

Time to say goodbye for now,
but the fun has just begun.

You are in the Kindness Club,
'cos it's for everyone!

For Alex, Ellie, Ru and Fern.
– K.B-C.

For all of you who are
kind … and love chickens
as much as I do. – D.P.

Bright Light
an imprint of
Hardie Grant Children's Publishing
Wurundjeri Country
Ground Floor, Building 1, 658 Church Street
Richmond, Victoria 3121, Australia

www.hardiegrantchildrens.com

A catalogue record for this
book is available from the
National Library of Australia

Hardie Grant acknowledges the Traditional Owners of the country on which we work, the Wurundjeri people
of the Kulin nation and the Gadigal people of the Eora nation, and recognises their continuing connection to the land,
waters and culture. We pay our respects to their Elders past and present.

9781761210440 (hbk)

Designed by Pooja Desai
Printed in China by Leo Paper Group

5 4 3